75 for the 75th

A Selected: 2002-2020

David P Reiter

Interactive Press

Brisbane

Interactive Press
an imprint of IP (Interactive Publications Pty Ltd)
Treetop Studio • 9 Kuhler Court
Carindale, Queensland, Australia 4152
sales@ipoz.biz
ipoz.biz/IP/IP.htm

First published by IP in 2022
extracts from *My Planets: a fictive memoir* (© 2011), *Timelord Dreaming*)
(© 2015); *Time Lords Remixed: a Dr Who poetical* (© 2020)

Printed in 12 pt Adobe Caslon Pro on 16 pt Avenir Book.

ISBN 9781922332851 (PB); ISBN 97819-22332868 (eBook)

A catalogue record for this book is available from the National Library of Australia

Interactive Press
75 for the 75th

Dr David P. Reiter is an award-winning poet and writer of fiction, and CEO of IP, an innovative print and digital publisher in Brisbane. His fourth book, *Hemingway in Spain and Selected Poems*, was shortlisted for the Adelaide Festival Awards. His previous books include *The Cave After Saltwater Tide* (Penguin, 1994) for which he won the Queensland Premier's Poetry Award. His book of short fiction, *Triangles*, was shortlisted for the Steele Rudd Award. Other works are *The Gallery*, interactive multimedia; *Kiss and Tell, Selected and New Poems 1987-2002*; and *Sharpened Knife*, a multimedia murder mystery. IP released his novel *Liars and Lovers* in 2003. His script, *Paul & Vincent*, was broadcast by ABC Radio National, followed by the release of a multimedia version from IP Digital, based on his poetry book *Letters We Never Sent*. He's completed a film and audiobook of *Hemingway in Spain*. *Real Guns* is a children's picture book illustrated by Irish artist Patrick Murphy. His *Project Earth-mend* Series of four children's books includes *The Greenhouse Effect*, *Global Cooling*, *Tiger Tames the Min Min* and *Tiger Takes the Big Apple*. He won the Wesetern Australian Premier's Award for *Timelord Dreaming* (2016) and *My Planets: a fictive Memoir* (2012). His most recent works are the digital narrative *Black Books Publishing* (2018) and *Time Lords Remixed: a Dr Who poetical* (2020).

David has had several grants from the Australia Council and Arts Queensland and has been writer-in-residence at a number of places including the Banff Centre for the Arts, Bundanon (the Arthur Boyd property), the Michael King Centre in New Zealand, and the Katharine Susannah Prichard Centre in Perth, Western Australia.

Interactive Press

Brisbane

Contents

from **My Planets:**
a fictive memoir

Foreword

The nature of a "fictive memoir" as coined by the author depends on his fragmentary recollections and imagined reconstruction of events and personalities past and present based on his own reflection and the subjective views of others. The metaphor "my planets" underlines the difficulty of mediating a single "reality" between often conflicting recollections from various people. His method is as scientific and detached as possible, but he does not insist that the truth presented in the work is definitive. His is the problem faced by all people separated from their biological family at birth or early in their lives. The "truth" they strive for in redefining their identity will always be tentative and subjective. But the journey between planets is necessary if they are ever to achieve a reconciliation between what was lost in the past and the dangling threads of the present.

Mercury

Look Up

Mercury can only be seen at twilight, and only then if you know where to look.

I was always attracted to twilight when I was a boy. Summer was a magical time. Fireflies arose from nowhere just as the noise of the city began to fade with the heat. In winter, snowflakes faded to grey before being freshened by streetlamps.

One twilight, the man I knew as my father took me out with a Palomar telescope he'd bought me for my seventh birthday. The largest mirror, at the base of a plastic cylinder, caught the image of the planet, and reflected it on to a smaller mirror, which bounced it onto the lens. So you saw only the apparition of your target as a cooling light wave.

Mercury *was* small, but I did make it out through the telescope, once. It was a quivering violin string for seconds before vanishing into the darkness.

I pestered my father to find Mercury for me again, but he refused. He doubted that I had seen it at all. Venus and Mars and even Jupiter were easier, he said. For Mercury, you had to be in the right place at the right time. My father thought himself unlucky. And I guess he saw no reason to dwell on it by pursuing Mercury night after night.

Until he passed it on his way to the stars.

Mercury in 3D

Apollo is the son you'd bring home to mother. He studies hard, doesn't do drugs, escapes the Draft lottery, and becomes a doctor like all good Jewish boys. A specialist, even. He's much better with money than you, buys shares before the Bull, sells before the Bear. He trashes the little he had to learn about the Holocaust and wishes that others would do the same. Getting even is a fatter bank account, and imagination is the shortest path to bronze.

Hermes is the null to his cross. He played hard, did every drug he could scrounge, never registered for the Draft, and shortened the straightest line between college and a pay slip. He becomes an IT specialist – that is, he flogs barcode readers to merchants who think "dpi" stands for Department of Primary Industries. He keeps his money unrolled and doesn't mind when it dissolves in his fingers. He will watch a Holocaust video on his cellular phone with a widescreen attitude. He knows that imagination means market share, so he buys it fresh, at full retail.

Vulcan is the chink in their armor. Scientists blame him for the tic in Apollo's cheek, and Hermes' larrikin streak. Microcephalic at birth, due to brutal forceps, he was excused from study, ignored by the Draft, and content enough to conspire in tongues with the other vegetables. Some of his best doctors are German and he is grateful for any attention the Holocaust and anything else brings him. He is pure imagination, and finds it a warm word under the stars.

Boiler Room

The apartment we rented on East Overlook was in the basement. You had to enter from the back of the apartment block, down some wrought iron stairs, then you came to a security door at the base, with the stench of garbage from a chute open to the upper floors. The overhead light bulbs hadn't been dusted for years.

The walls of the hallway were rendered brick that must have been whitewashed ages ago, and the floor was smooth concrete, painted bright ochre. On your right, you passed a laundry room, with coin-operated machines that ran from dawn to dusk, and then, just across from our apartment door, the boiler room.

The door to the boiler room was kept shut, but, in the winter, you could still hear it rumbling away like a rocket engine getting up the nerve to blast off. Some kids on the upper floors reckoned it was fuelled with the carcasses of rats and stray cats, but further investigations revealed it was oil heating the water that produced the steam that sputtered through the radiators in the apartments. Not that we needed our radiators: the boiler was close enough to heat our unit by simple convection.

It was a place that Dickens and even Dante could have drawn inspiration from, and I hated it. I heard my mother cry some nights when she thought I was asleep lying on the bed next to hers, and I knew why. The Fates had dealt us a bad hand. The only thing worse than being a young widow was being a *poor* one.

We had a roof over our heads, but only just. You could not see the stars at night. In winter, the window wells filled with snow. Like a glacier nudging your shoulder.

There was no place to go from East Overlook except out on the street and, hopefully, up.

Venus

My Evening Star

Venus. *Venus*. Some nights I would escape from our flat to a park with trees that blocked out the street lights just so I could gaze up at her. How could she be a planet *and* the Evening Star? A goddess veiled in gases that were beautiful from afar but poison to anyone who ventured too close.

I imagined her as my birth mother. Watching over me before fading into a dark hood of stars. She'd made her choice, but her secret would be safe with me.

She was pure art before the thunder. And she had not forgotten me.

Venus had no moons, so I wanted to believe my mother had no other children. She would know better than to disturb a perfect dream.

Dancing Sinatra

I have to pinch myself. Here I am, about to knock on Frank Sinatra's door at 2am. I don't know what to expect. No, I *do* know what to expect, but I'm still here!

He's promised me the last dance. In his room. The top floor in the Ritz Hotel. Will there be room for the band, too, or will we hum a slow dance cheek-to-cheek?

I put my ear to the door and hear…nothing. Is that a good sign?

When I knock, a tall man opens the door. He's a bit of a grease-ball, very handsome and muscle-bound, but he's not Frankie.

I look around him, into the dim.

'Come in, Miss,' he says politely. 'The boss is expecting you.'

Where *is* the boss?' I ask, wondering if this is Frankie's room at all.

'On his way,' the man says, walking inside. 'My name's Reg. I'm to look after you until he gets here.'

'And how long is that likely to be… Reg?' I say, following him.

'As long as it takes,' he says. 'Hungry?'

There's the faint smell of Italian food lingering in the air.

What's that smell?' I ask.

'Eggplant Parmigiana,' he says. 'Frankie made it, especially for you.'

'Oh, really,' I say. 'And when would he have done that – between acts?'

This morning,' Reg says, trying to stifle the grin. 'Don't know how he knew you was coming but he did!'

'Lots of garlic?' I say, playing along.

Reg rubs an imaginary bit between his thumb and

forefinger. 'Only the smallest bit, in the tomato sauce. Frankie's a genius with Parmesan!'

'I'll bet you say that to all the girls!' I say.

'Only the ones he cooks for!' he winks. 'Want some?'

I nod and sink into a chair. It smells like perfume. Fresh perfume.

He was right about the parmigiana. Two glasses of champagne later, still no Frankie, and Reg is getting *very* friendly.

'What if Frankie comes in?' I say, trying to hold him off.

'Something tells me,' Reg murmurs, 'that he's been held up. But I can pass on the good word for you – in the morning.'

By then, I was so tired that, Frankie or Reg, it hardly made any difference. And Reg didn't seem to mind the garlic on my breath.

Magellan Flirts With Venus

I am proof that adventure
is still the booster rocket of myth
yet only small change at the foot
of a goddess.

You watched me tack my way here
reading the furrows of solar wind
until my auto-phase in Mission Control
steered me into respectful orbit

and I *want* a touch-down to danger
after you scatter the clouds between
your knees, promising to dismiss
your bodyguards, freeing us
to do what mortals can only
dream of in evening star phase.

The hormones surge on
long after the worms have finished
so my anodized skin won't let us
down when your heat begins to bite.

Or is this just my dizzy solar cells
making fun of bronze?

Earth

Earth Talk

It's a lot to ask of a minor planet. It wasn't my choice to be a safe house for life in all of its fits and starts. I'd prefer to be alone, and some day I still hope to be. I conjure up storms, floods, plagues – even asteroids – but no one packs their bags. If only their priests spoke a single language, they could hear their fate ticking away.

Orphans, children in detention? Yes, I feel sorry for them. But poverty is a state of mind, and I have seen those who have known ecstasy from an extra crust tossed at their feet. Pure science and art are an act of ego not family. So be grateful for friction and get on with your future!

Affinity

Joni Mitchell sang *you don't know what you've got till it's gone*, but what's the loss when you never knew what you had?

I had no idea who my parents were, why they gave me up, what they looked like, how they felt the instant, hour, day, month, year, decade, lifetime after they gave me up. Or whether I should be bothered about it.

All around me, children would say *daddy* or *mommy* and mean it. Their sense of belonging needed no filters, no translation.

Imagine being born without skin and then, frame-by-frame, watching someone grease it on you like strips of wallpaper.

They took more notice of recall than genes back then. Keep the slate wet, so the chalk will skip, smearing the evidence. Make sure the light is bright enough to dance planets before his eyes, distracting him from any thought of litigation.

Parents are not as reliable as statues. When the swallows return, the Lost Prince has gone.

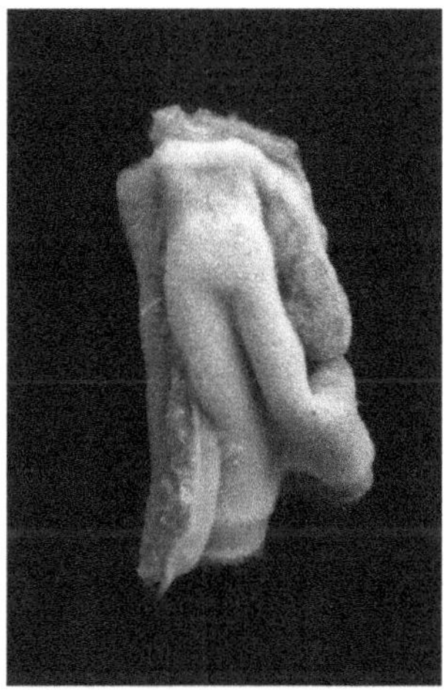

To Autumn

It was all grass when we bought it
as if green is enough to deny the drab.
That and a perfect square only made
rectangular by the prudent slice
of dedicated concrete off one edge.

It was the *idea* that mattered to you.
Scruff of the neck stuff, defining us
with deed. And without a husband
to enact your design, less perfection
wasted in compromise.

Nothing less than Jackson & Perkins
would do for roses. You took days
to choose. Not by hue but history:
petals to the manor born. Exertion
no object where my labor was free.

Bare roots arrived swathed in plastic.
With flags of moisture crying
take us to earthworms take us take us

Did I enjoy their limbo too much?
I laid them out in early morning sun
on the embankment like dank villagers
slain for politics, the scent of innocent
lives still clinging to their extremities.

I dug them in securely to flower
for your love. But you hardly noticed.

I will go back to visit some day.
Tear away insidious grass from fisted
collars, read Keats cross-legged on frost,
thinking how no impulse waits for spring.

Can you hear their jagged color now?

Mars

17

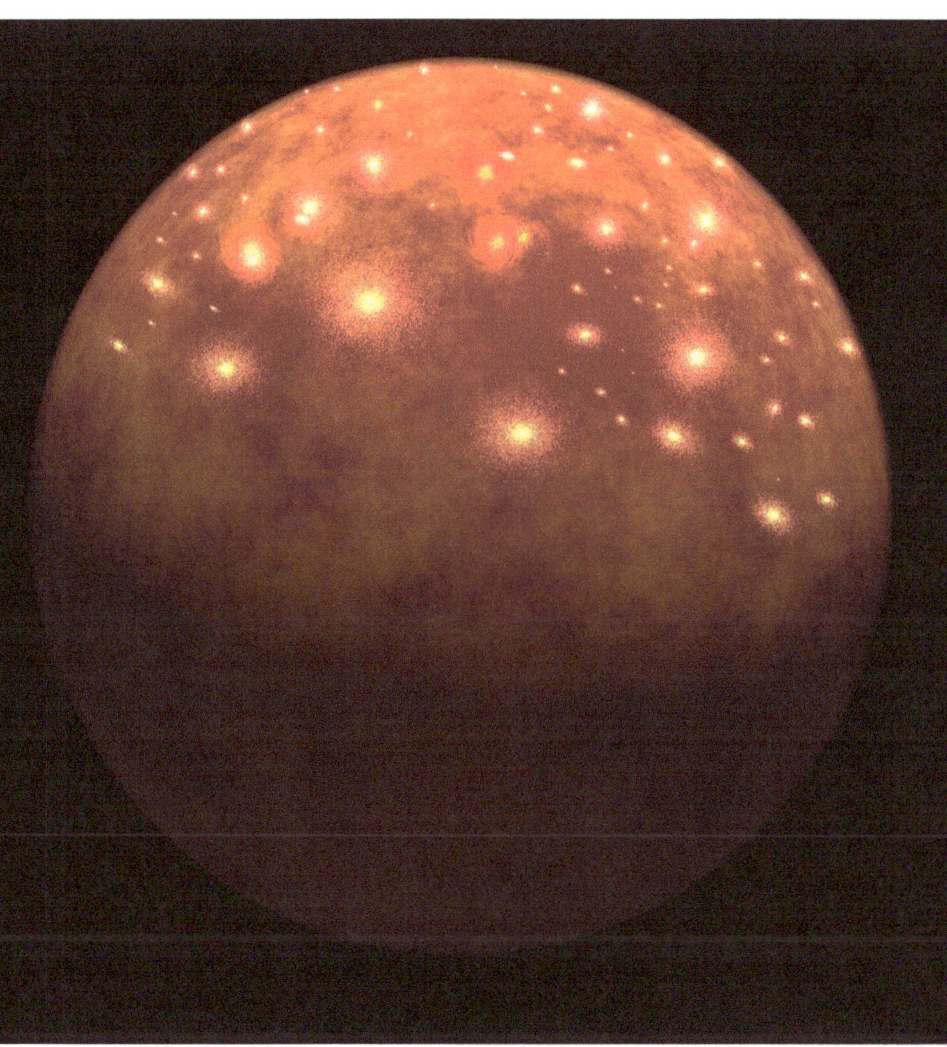

Mars

Divides

A scream rips through the night air. Soon after a pot shatters against a wall. I shiver, and will myself invisible under the sheets. The nightlight sputters like a candle in a sudden breeze. Mildew is rising on the air.

From here I hardly recognise their voices. Monsters spilling out from a nightmare closet. My mother's scream becoming an ultimatum. She is threat, he mere reaction, a fire hose to her spot-flames.

'If only…'

'I can't…'

I am the cause – someone else's child. That which should bond, tears apart.

On such a night, Jewish women packed their unbaked bread and waited for Moses to part the Red Sea. The children tested the seabed, watched by God, while their mothers worried.

Frieda stands in the glare of hall light, six shades of grey, seven with the blood she swabs away from her mouth. She has a determined suitcase.

'Say good-bye to your father,' she says as we move toward the front door where he stonewalls.

'I don't want to go!' I cry, burying my face in his thigh. 'It's all my fault – I'm *sorry*.'

Then he has us in his iron grip, one in each arm, and he's looming, solid and spreading like an ancient tree. He's Sampson, and my face is covered with cut hair.

My Masada

Not a mountain.
Or even a defiant stone.
Though I might have wished
it so.

Perspective can make you vanish
at any height if you are unexpected.

So my fortress was made of maple
and iron. The better to surprise.

Still, the power can threaten or punish
the young for what they don't
understand. Unless you diminish.

Of course you don't heed the call.
Scouts are marshaled to the scent
avenues scoured for accident
basements flooded with beams.
But at eye-level, not under-story.

Gran's sewing table was my premise.
A trademark neglected, so how could it
contain? I could taste their fear now
but a Maccabee's not made for mercy.

Let them wait.

Let the whole *world* wait.

Next I'll be Angel of the Lord
come to smite their first-born.
Or any others who cross me
before dinner-time!

Don't Shoot the Robot

I was under instructions:
sift the sand for water
find a narrative
in the canals

But the sand played dead
and the rocks gave me
the cold shoulder

It didn't help calling them
by Greek names
a dead Greek tells no lies
unless he writes for a living

What is this fascination we have
with ricocheting our inertia
onto others?

Here, the Valles Marineris
is a Ground Zero wider than America's
marble arias, a litany of bin ladens

OK. Water *may* have sculpted these rocks
while the Earth cooled – there,
does that make you feel any better?
But your science flies at half-mast, Carl[1],
and your doubts are showing.

[1] Sagan, the Astrophysicist

Jupiter

21

Settling the Score

I really don't know what all the fuss is about. Just because you live on a *solid*, you think Earth is the center of the universe. Well. You are nothing more than a speck to me, even when I am in stalemate with the Sun, my only rival in this solar system. I have storms that have lasted longer than your species.

I have fathered every myth of importance – and then some. But why should I partner with *mortals* about celestial design? I will bury all of your memories. Certainly after the smudge you have made of your temperate corner is long forgotten.

You make a big deal of war, as if other beings should give a jot about your push button deities. You kill, kill, kill to feed these daydreams and earn no thanks for your trouble. It's the price you pay for being American, a solitary flag-bearer to freedom.

The faster you spin out of control, the happier I am to let you blur into the stars.

Jupiter Man

After you imploded
After you abandoned me
I called you Jupiter, bringer of joy
And sang to you across the arid sky.

But the echoes I heard
Were my own refrains

Your translucent heart
cloudy eyes
tangled cocoon

In your parallel universe
You still care
But I can't reach your harmony

From here

No Gods Before Me

God had a scent long before I'd heard of religion. He was rainforest timber and royal blue seats. Tarnished silver polish and yellowed Torah. His Words falling away, pixels at a time.

I loved to watch the narrow windows of the synagogue slowly darken to azure with the Sabbath, and I tingled as the candles were lit. Other gods conspired beyond our cloister, but I knew that, one day, they would ask the True God to forgive them.

Though just the adopted son of a truck driver, I felt I would always be one of His Chosen, come what may. Money was no object. Social standing was a myth. We were one, under God, and had to do nothing but *be* to enjoy His blessing.

I used to lie awake in bed, talking to Him. He was listening – I was sure of that. Soon I would earn my burning bush.

'About my real parents…'

'What about them, my son?'

'Why didn't they want me?'

'Perhaps they were too young.'

'I'm not too young to miss them.'

'We must learn from the past, not regret it.'

'I should forgive them, then?'

'That's what the Bible says.'

'You have a quick answer for everything, don't you?'

'It comes with the territory, David. Now go to sleep…'

Saturn

25

Tween

Not in the brightest ring, or the fainter B Ring, or even the crepe inner one you need a decent telescope to see, I belonged to Cassini's Division, in the gap where unbought tickets wait to be redeemed. And wait.

I started backstage and never stole a kiss. I didn't have the clothes, the look, the space-walk. They could tell I was *interstellar* and not for touch.

You might detect me, up close. Or not. Just as quickly moving on to your next conquest.

The Rings of Saturn

Eileen smokes. She always has, ever since she can remember. She claims she *could* give it up if she wanted to, will, one of these days.

Frieda was even worse. She smoked whenever she could, as if making a point to the world. But it was *do as I say not as I do* when she caught me with one and her lighter back of the garage one day. I was seven, and she was furious.

She forced me to smoke it until I threw up. Handed me a tissue and then walked away.

She probably knew she was killing herself by slow degree even before the Surgeon-General's warnings became fashionable. She might have asked for a cigarette on her deathbed if hospital protocol had allowed it. She'd done her duty and raised a son; now she could get on with her death.

Eileen can see a meteorite with her name on it hurtling toward Earth, but she too can't care less. Though she does make allowances by only smoking outdoors, or in the tiny bathroom off the laundry.

I tell her 'You could fly to Australia on what you spend on cigarettes and dog food for those raccoons.'

It gives her pause, but only briefly.

Richard says 'Hey, if your mother farts in that tiny little room while she's lighting up, she might get enough of a boost to fly halfway to the moon!'

It's a vintage Richard-ism, so I offer a charitable laugh. We non-smokers can use all the friends we can get.

Miranda Personified

When the magic wears off, you're left with nothing but rocks and ice. South Sea islands and shipwrecks attract few moguls these days, and when you take off your clothes to lie spread-eagled in the sand, it's always some Caliban who creeps up to service you. Forget what Ariel whispered in your ear: all the passion comes *before* marriage.

What's left to explore once every part of your body has been pierced with gold? You dream in designer drugs now, the more expensive the better. You exploded to the core once, but learned your lesson – have Photoshop, will travel.

You're three hundred miles across now… and counting.

Neptune

29

Soundings

There must have been many baths
but this is the only one I remember
with you:

my clothes in a pile on the scuffed lino,
how you had to boost me over the lip
of the old cast-iron tub to the suds

the water that stung until I settled
back between your legs. This
was father and son, one of few

signposts that memory flashes
before the static forces you to switch
channels. And what we did

in the water as it slicked with grease.
Those cuts and bruises on your legs –
they were male courage, so when

could I expect mine? You laughed.
'If I work long enough, you'll miss 'em
and earn a doctor's smooth hands!

I tried to laugh your deep laugh.
'But I want *your* hands. I want to work
just like you!' You hushed me.

'Your mother won't have it,' you said,
'and she's probably right.' But you let me
soap your back and rub away some death

from your broken skin in those frames
when I was sure you would live forever
before the water suddenly cooled.

Fear of Horses

Their height. Their strength. Their mystery. Motors had dropped them in favour of myths, so how could I think of riding one?

I could watch Zorro, and admire his flare with lightning bolts, but I couldn't pick out Pegasus in the sky. Some constellations depend on more than a steady eye and faith.

Bellerophon would have won the Kentucky Derby in his day, but he paid the price for testing Zeus' patience.

When you're fatherless, no one offers you a boost up into the stirrups to chance your life with a headstrong beast. But I preferred to walk at my pace and be splattered with their clay.

I didn't miss the lather. Or the sweaty risk.

Hosing

You can see everything but the heat
in that old photo of me and my first Dad.

There were five concrete steps
up to the porch where we'd sit
with the scent of meat and gravy
lingering on the evening air.

It was a time of silence,
watching the sun click down
from smoky reds to purples
until a night blanket stirred the crickets

while Dad arced his hose
in figure-eights over the lawn.
'Make me a rainbow,' I'd beg.
He was all I knew of magic back then.

His lips would tighten as he said
rainbows couldn't be bothered
with the son of a poor man
unless he spoke like a gentleman.

So I sang somewhere over the rainbow
way up high there's a land that I've heard of
and he'd brush it in with a sweep of his wrist
and I'd dance in the mist he raised

to find his pot of gold, but it vanished
before I could bring it back.
Then the fireflies began to tease me
and I'd follow him like a cub

while he soaked the brick walls
and concrete path until they were
cool enough for me to sleep.
I can't remember sweating in bed

at all on those sticky nights
when my father made it rain.

75 for the 75th

Pluto

35

Snowpath

The boy has dreamt this:

igloo – a clean sculpt of knife on brick
sweet burn of driftwood for body heat
sizzle of salmon in the pan
yellow eyes pacing the margins.

But no such metaphors this far south –
here snowfall has a clock of its own
and a sudden dump may trigger a thaw.
So the boy is ready when it comes.

At first light he's stamping out
an arterial to magnetic north
retracing, sliding sideways
to harden the path. Even as

the snow tries to overwrite
his sketches with sculpted drifts
but he has an instinct for the brittle
under powder and ploughs on

smoothing, banking to speed,
gauging the lesson of snow fence,
no thought of friends still asleep
to avoid the nuisance of cold.

His mother's last call to breakfast
is a drizzle beyond the white-out
and no easy cave will distract him now
from that stench of wolf just ahead.

Sugar Shacks

This is all I remember of spring when I was young.
A grey day, and my father scrapping a skiff of ice
off the windscreen of the Oldsmobile. Inside
I scratch the glass with my fingernails to see out
and shavings of frost feather down onto my lap.
My mother lights another cigarette and chides me
for taking off my mittens, her words scudding
in white puffs that sting my eyes. 'You'll catch
your death,' she says and I imagine the sting of it
like a baseball you snare with your bare hands.

My father clambers inside, and the sun comes out.
Our wheels spin but then take hold in the glistening
thaw. 'How many miles will it be to the sugar shack?'
I ask him. 'Don't be so impatient,' says my mother,
'or we'll turn back!' But my father makes up a song
through the slushy city and then the sleepy farms
until we see the maple trees along the Chardon...

Skeins of steam drift over us and I can smell
boiling sap from the log cabins down the path.
'Those are sugar shacks,' my father says, 'and this
is how you taste them.' He scoops up a fistful
of snow, pats it into a ball and hands it to me.
In the first cabin a man in a lumberjack shirt
is stoking the fire under a trough of dark liquid.
He takes the snowball and dips it in hot syrup
then shows us how to gently tap a tree for sap.
'Doesn't it hurt when the trunk bleeds?' I ask.
'Only when we do it without respect,' he says.

My father died late that autumn. He'd masked
the illness from me, though my mother must

have known as he joked about his chalky skin.
He'd never read about how rain can burn the soil,
scarring roots, nor see green leaves go brittle
in the dry cough of summer while the sap's pulse
slows. A world away I wonder if a man still tends
those coals, waiting for the first taste of blame
to bubble into the thickening syrup. Or has his
sooty cabin already slumped into melting snow?

Kol Nidre

The rabbis could argue – all I cared about was the music and Cantor Bushman's singing in the candlelight. *He* knew what it meant, and that was enough for me. I assumed it had something to do with death and forgiveness, and that was all I needed to know. The best music cleanses you without trying.

But at that first Yom Kippur service after my father's death, I couldn't keep the tears from my eyes. The rabbi would read his name during his roll call of those who had died from the congregation in the past year, and though I knew the saying of it would be indistinguishable from the rest I was still disappointed when the rabbi failed to pause, even briefly. This was what a life came to, a shooting star in dry syllables.

Suddenly, I was 'man of the house', at twelve years of age.

My father's heart failed him on the Fourth of July, and the fireworks continued unabated as the ambulance, adding its red slashes into the muted star-scape, droned its way to the hospital. He lingered on, like a final chord from a distracted organist, then joined the list.

It's said that the *Kol Nidre* prayer forgives you in advance for all the vows of the coming year that you'll fail to realize. It's much more pragmatic and fatalist than going to confession, but the bottom line is the same: the slate's rubbed clean, with a musty rag, and you feel better for it.

I lit a candle for him on the anniversary of his death and did my best to sing the prayer over it in an unwavering voice. The candle lasted more than a day, but it was no Chanukah miracle, and I was no match for a Maccabee.

What my mother never saw was me burning my finger on the flame in the middle of the night, as I tried to summon Charon. I'd followed my father everywhere, so how could he leave me to pace the bank of such a river for a hundred years?

My skin has healed, the organ plays on.

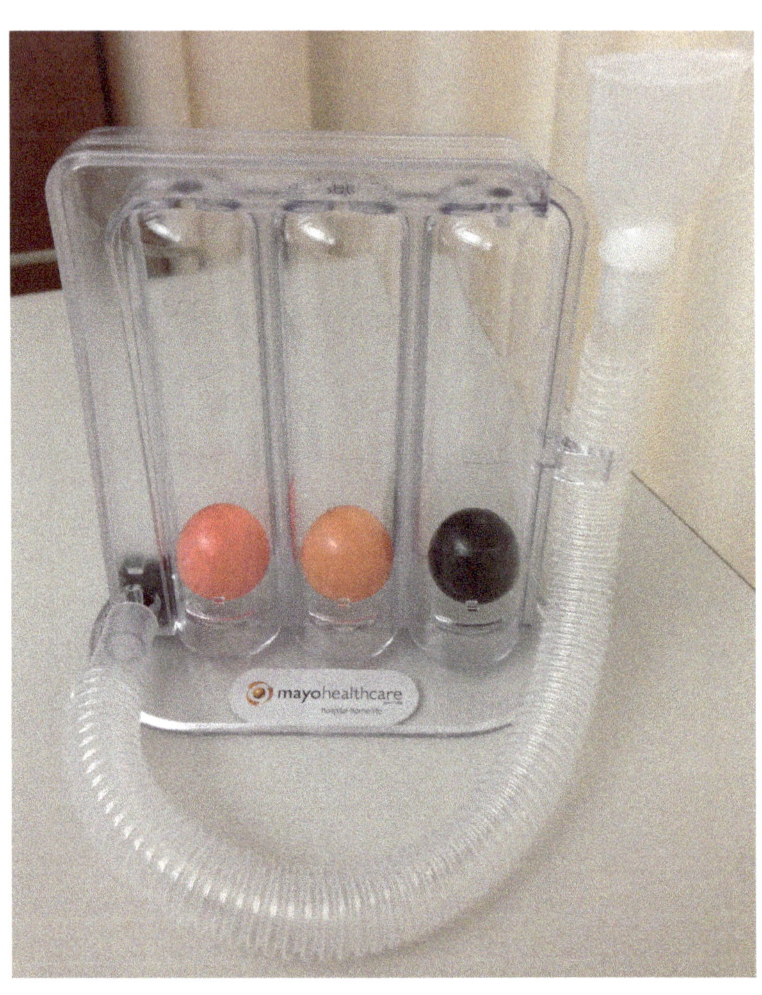

from Timelord Dreaming: tweetems from ward 8b
(2015)

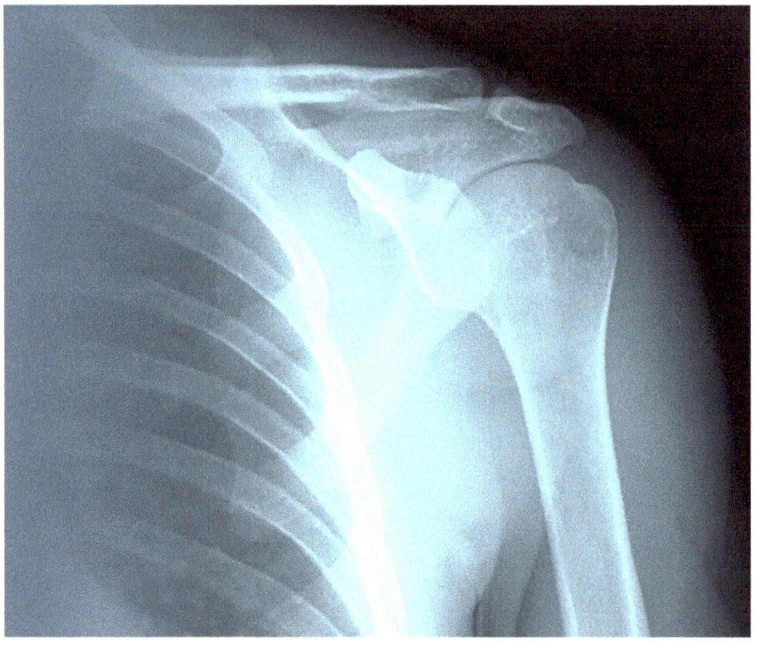

Foreword

Hospital stays are usually the stuff of clichés. If you're lucky enough to survive your stay in Emergency and get admitted for observation or an operation, and are public enough about your situation, people will take note and chat with and about you. Social media makes it so much easier to document your journey from arrival to departure and points beyond, and for people to share your experiences. Often these will be friends or close acquaintances, but sometimes they'll be "friends" you've admitted to your network for whatever reason who identify with your circumstances enough to message you for all to see.

As a patient, you feel your identity slipping away the longer you remain in hospital. And the older you are, the more likely you'll be called 'love' or 'dear' by time-poor nurses and orderlies. In the artificial light and the drip-haze of medication, time and the senses blur and surreality takes hold. The mind tries to latch onto fragments of the familiar and even these dissolve without a drug free effort to capture them.

I decided to invent a new form to recreate and reflect on these fragments, what I call the *tweetem*. It's a cross between Japanese forms like the tanka and the character-limited tweet. Each tweetem must be self-contained, with a kick in the tail at the end, in 140 characters or less. Whether or not this new form endures, or is even tolerated from the beginning to the ending of the work at hand is up to you.

The overall narrative is under compression, as I've said, but it has the kinetic potential to expand associatively if you pursue the many hyperlinks (diversions) offered. This is easier if you're viewing the digital version but still rewarding if you've opted for the physical book and have an Internet device at hand.

And, yes, the Timelord I met in the haze and half-light *was* real, and I trust that he will one day sidestep out of his parallel universe long enough to meet his more infamous *other*.

999.3

'Please scale your [#pain](http://tinyurl.com/pytqko9)[1] from 1 to 10.

We sustain for the EW – no exits on our watch.

Name, date of birth, allergies – best to *memorise*.'

---

[1] http://tinyurl.com/pytqko9

4D Print from the #TARDIS[1]

#Dr Who[2] at the EW shapeshifts for the transfer,

blue jab in my bowels, #centrifuge[3] of max focus

betrayed by a tease of dancing lights.

---

[1] http://tinyurl.com/mrrdfyt

[2] http://tinyurl.com/olxvwz8

[3] https://twitter.com/centrifugemusic

EW – Sunday, midnight

'Excluded your heart. Now for the shadows.

My [4]#sonic screwdriver will scan for #aliens.[5]'

Yes, my pain is there, and *there* – a solid 8.

---

[4] http://youtu.be/LXliD189bss
[5] http://tinyurl.com/kowam3n

Blood secret business

Need to know? Even in theatre, privacy comes first.

Tubes, needles, incisions deal out their clichés.

Somewhere, your [6]#universal donor sighs.

---

[6] http://tinyurl.com/naev53g

#<u>Dalek</u>[7] lock-on – Monday, 01:00hrs

You are now locked on to our sensors.

Your frail flesh and synapses *will* obey.

Have you scrubbed for your [#gods](#)?[8]

---

[7] http://tinyurl.com/klr39mx

[8] http://tinyurl.com/og6c4qe

The Watchtower – 04:00

Stainless #CareFusion[9] tattles in my stats

throbbing red at each flow dip or interrupt –

I grapple for the green pulse of a call button

---

[9] http://tinyurl.com/pbe2l9k

Dr Who to ultra – 07:30

Fresh from janitor skin at Clara's school

Dr Who hushes me with a aging finger –

#Mercury,[10] not #Charon,[11] tonight for my tests

---

10 http://wordinfo.info/unit/3814/ip:6/il:M

11 http://tinyurl.com/psqzeym

My #endone goddess[12]

Detours from a plastic cup, minimalist,

slightly sweaty in off-white coatings

to sleep #perchance to nightmare[13] … of you

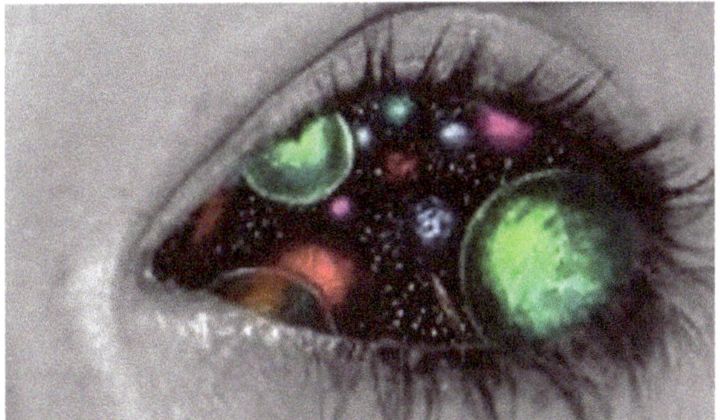

State of play – 10:05

#Ultrasound:[14] *something's in there*

X-Ray: *50ml fluid on the right lung*

Bloods: #recalcitrant[15] *kidney & liver*

---

[14] http://tinyurl.com/m86bxpu
[15] http://quitegoodcomics.com/

Thin **#red laser**[16]

Is your ally, so *relax*, sip the air

until safely inside its whirring batcave

Your cells #gently deconstructed[17]

[16] http://youtu.be/269BLY_gJ74
[17] http://tinyurl.com/k5f8etb

"Crack your cheeks…"

I ponder what [#Lear](http://tinyurl.com/m5wrsmu)[18] must have felt

forsaken by daughters on that icy heath

but then a warm blanket for my countdown

---

[18] http://tinyurl.com/m5wrsmu

#Short-term loss[19]

I don't remember: the tube slithering

down my throat, the interrogations,

snips, bleed, metal plug, seal, #curtain call[20]

---

[19] http://tinyurl.com/mxo7u9a
[20] http://youtu.be/SLbuUQ-RNGg

White bread at dawn

A sure signature of #resurrection[21]

with butter, strawberry jam and tea

Rolled oats waits for no tongue

---

[21] http://tinyurl.com/lz4cpvn

Little surprises

Specialist hardens into focus, junior doctors
at heel. 'In the nick of time,' he says, fatherly,
'your gallbladder was #gangrenous!'[22]

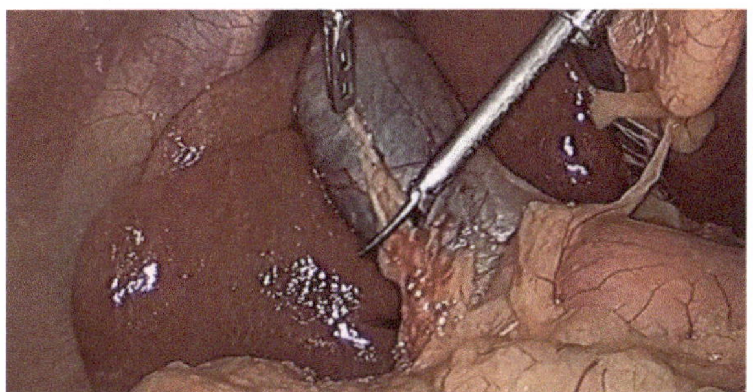

---

[22] http://tinyurl.com/qeb2bkz

Who needs pay tv

In the arterial twilight of the corridor

Dr Who deploys a #maximalist[23] script

#denying his lust[24] for spunky Clara

---

23 http://tinyurl.com/nd4k87r
24 http://tinyurl.com/9fkyrx

A poem in it

[#Nil by mouth](25), nil by page, nil by life

– no inmate roadblocks to reflection –

dreamscapes transition to parole

---

25 http://tinyurl.com/m4v32dr

Breathless

My #Incentive Spirometer[26] is #counter-intuitive[27]:

inhale to blow three coloured balls spaceward

red, easy; orange, maybe; black, stubborn

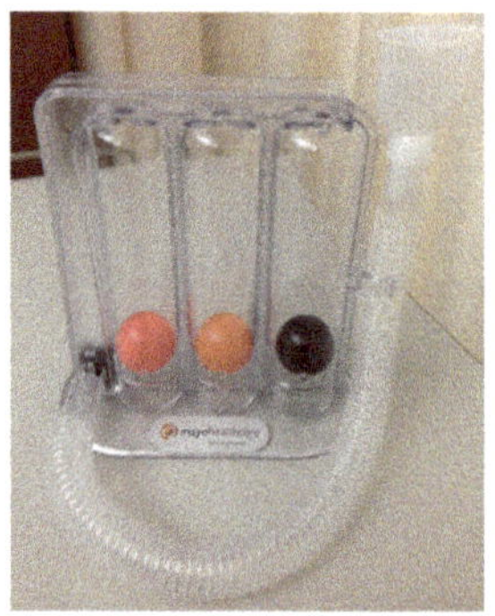

---

[26] http://tinyurl.com/jw4388s
[27] http://tinyurl.com/khantpa

Splendid solitary

One faecal test was all it took

to unmask a selfie [#superbug](http://tinyurl.com/8mxn7)[28]

consigning me to a private cell

---

[28] http://tinyurl.com/8mxn7

Negative increments

Superstition says *don't ask* for release

Pride comes before a [#relapse](https://vine.co/tags/TheRelapseSymphony)[29]

and the specialist of course knows best

---

[29] https://vine.co/tags/TheRelapseSymphony

Tardis awaits

At the [#cavalier flash](#)[30] of my medicare card

the crosshairs refresh for a grayscale landing pad

as Dr Who teleports into a new episode

---

[30] vimeo.com/78293068

Gravity

If scabs are your only #parachute[31]

plan your #identity removal[32] with care

or your dreams will weep with acid

---

[31] https://www.tumblr.com/tagged/parachute
[32] http://tinyurl.com/ow8e2g6

Foreign objects

So the ghost of my gallbladder is sealed

with a #titanium clip,[33] just the right size

to #prevent migration[34] and dribbles of bile

Harmonic objects

Given my druthers, I'd have chosen a slice

via #Harmonic Scalpel[35], which seals

as it dissects with shuffled, sterile iTunes.

---

[35] http://tinyurl.com/kgm5xx7

Dr Who skates on

Between night shifts, he films an #Arctic

episode[36] with ironic glances at Camera 1

I share – *get on with it, mate, Life that is*

My parallel universe

Before: a shard of bronzed immortality

After: an epiphany at my [#instant of thaw](37)

Synchronies aligned to a discord of time

---

from Time Lords Remixed: a Dr Who poetical (2020)

Foreword

Think of what you are about to read as a poetic Tardis that lands on the page then teleports to the limits of your imagination – via the Internet and beyond. It focuses primarily on the most recent episodes from Series 8 through 12 but occasionally references earlier legacy works.

I'm "writing back" to the episodes by creating a version of the Doctor's voice, and reflecting key beats and phrases to create a remixed version. This is in keeping with the literary nature of the *Dr Who* series, building on its poetic and allusive potentials.

There are two distinct recast voices here: Peter Capaldi, the 12th Doctor, and Jodie Whittaker's 13th . My interest in Capaldi's Doctor began with the slightly medicated experiences I had that led to the writing of Timelord Dreaming. I've been fascinated by the debate that raged around the appearance of the first female Doctor, so we have a very different voice for Series 11, which brings us up to the end of 2019 from the first referenced Series 8 episode in 2014.

To create "multiverse" and engaged effects, I associated freely on the Internet, cross-referencing sites that I felt added documentary or artistic dimensions to themes sounded by the poetic voices. With the physical version, you need to copy and paste the footnote links at the bottom of the page into a browser; with the digital versions, you can simply "mouse-over" and click on the hyperlinked text, or click on the relevant footnote. As a post-modern reader, you have the choice of interacting with the hyperlinks or not – or even extending your personal multiverse by going with the flow of suggested links offered by the hosting sites.

– David P Reiter

Series 8

Minerva: Next Contact

My spidercam[1] has found intelligent
life is a more difficult question
than an answer

I launch a swarm
of curious robots
to whisper in alien

algorithms that test
Drake's Equation of deliberate
fractions[2] for the right planet

at the right time, burbling
in signatures of gold dust
gas and sodium. Do they

recall that Cambrian Explosion
that made predation an art
and evolution our paintbrush?

Should we scramble our radio
signals to camouflage false icons
like the Gorgon[3] or emerging

extinctions? My robots bleep
'no'. We are here to discover
not to be disrobed.

---

[1] rebrand.ly/da313
[2] rebrand.ly/k8usoo
[3] rebrand.ly/8um0ps

Into the Dalek

I've been holding Clara's coffee cup for only
a millisecond but it's gone polar – why?
As Aristotle, that Big Fella probe, gets rocked

not by Socrates, but a Dalek mother ship
simmering with her brood in the asteroid belt.
Dalek Rusty's[4] my recurring nightmare, so evil

he's morphed into good – moral, even –
though, when pushed, he excuses
morality as an engineering malfunction.

To analyse his algorithms we miniaturise
for the most dangerous, sludgy backstreets
of the universe, tricking his antibodies

to find the triadic leak that's compelling
him to babble on about beauty in a star –
until I've triggered him to reconfigure:

exterminate! – *EXTERMINATE!!*
Was I a good man before your slap, Clara,
or a better Dalek? The Master[5] would preach

that Daleks are works-in-revision, just like
Heaven – an endless star-trail to perfection.
And how could a time lord become a good *man*?

Not for a lack of strumming![6]

----

[4] rebrand.ly/nlfode
[5] rebrand.ly/xopbff
[6] rebrand.ly/h8opaq

Listen

Why do people talk aloud
when they know they're alone,
skipping heartbeats in the dark?[7]

Thinking you're awake when the cupboard
of your mind is shadowed, crowded with
outlines from the replicate nightmare

that shivers us back to a unison childhood:
the creaking of mattress springs as we lie
stock-still; the untranslatable groans

of the floorboards echoing our worst fears;
and then the speechless form that rises
under the chilled blanket of our silence.

I whisper at shadow-beings prone to hide
behind the banging pipes[8] of our doubts.
What phrases will they riddle to

bon voyage the lingering humans left
in the universe? But Clara, as usual,
invokes a wisdom to calm: it's me, young,

my back to her, trying to fend off my mantle
as future time lord. "Fear," she says, stroking
my sweaty scalp, "doesn't have to make you

---

[7] rebrand.ly/0nra5i
[8] rebrand.ly/74igv2

cruel. Fear can make you kind!" Though I usually <u>rankle at orders</u>,[9] I'll do as I'm told and accept that uncertainty as our constant,

in the Tardis that makes dark companions
of us
all.

---

[9] rebrand.ly/2rdux7

The Caretaker

Have you noticed how polished the Tardis
always is? Somewhere there's a robot
in autonomous HEPA mode,[10] camera-shy

between the bluster and choke of vortices.
It's easy to disguise your pixels with a sonic
when Danger's shouting *problem solution*

destroy so loud that even a Mistress can tune in
from The Promised Land. So I mimic under
deep cover at Clara's Coal Hill School[11]

with the wink of my eyebrows and an attentive
broom. 'John Smith' – how invisible is that?
It's not my style to sponge down walls, but

you do what you have to do to buffer
the planet. And Clara from that somersaulting
PE teacher Mr Pink, aka Orson, aka Rupert

who thinks *he* saved us from Skovox Blitzer[12]
(she really could do much better than an ex-
soldier who pretends to teach Math). But

who am I – her lost-and-found Daddy?
Yes, there has been a certain spillage
of trust between dates, the aftertaste

from that first
mortal
kiss.

---

[10] rebrand.ly/5nonlt

[11] rebrand.ly/3b9crl

[12] rebrand.ly/fif8au

Mummy on the Orient Express

When two freebies for the Orient Express
stop the clock after that phone call, I can't resist
summoning my inner Poirot.[13] And what better way

to end the flirt by first-class with Clara, champagne
and silk pyjamas! Of course, with Agatha there's
always a cost: murders by a bubblewrap mummy

only the Doomed can see as Foretold[14] then just sixty-six
seconds before Promised Land Station. No unhinged
celebs or hard-light holograms are required for upload

and definitely no time for teleporters to duck away
from the bullet at their head. Your suspects will vary
from stale to putrid but you still must choose wisely

even after a white flag douses your addiction to war.[15]
Now Clara's smiling again, and I'm sure she's genuine:
"Shut up and give us a new planet!"

[13] rebrand.ly/0e3a2z
[14] rebrand.ly/oiomcq
[15] rebrand.ly/t9e7uu

Flatline

Let me enjoy just one moment of not
knowing – it happens so rarely! – while
my Tardis shrinks by dimensional leaching

into siege-mode toy for that Doctor of Lies:
Clara, of course! Luckily, I've hacked her optic
nerve so she's not entirely at free-range

to repel the Boneless[16] 2-Dems who're injecting
tradie lives into faceless murals. See how
polished she aims my sonic: "*I'm* the Doctor!"

Now, lying may be an essential survival skill[17]
in love and war, but that's taking license too far!
Still, as that Boneless crew morphs into 3Ds

she recruits a fluorescent pudding brain boy
to spray-paint a phantom train, ricocheting
their energy, while I finger-walk the Tardis
deftly across the tracks in an *Addams Family*[18]

meme. Monsters banished, I have to concede she
was exceptional. Goodness had nothing
to do with it.

---

[16] rebrand.ly/oq7nrq
[17] rebrand.ly/wth8u3
[18] rebrand.ly/5fdm8m

In the Forest of the Night

Mining embers from the poet to stir up a forest
posse: trunks no thicker than a single ring swaddle
London overnight, while a rampant Tyger roars

in mid-air to leap over iron spikes[19] into oblivion.
Young Maebh waves away the expel of solar flares.
And Maebh waves away[20] the not-impossible wolves

her elders deny. While Earth braces for an invasion
the speechless deserve, trees give voice to a page
before stars imploded and an epilogue after the solar

fusion that translated into our Sun. But forests can
forgive for the planet's sake, not of its human layer,
and they disperse the flares by withholding the breath

that would have incinerated the lifeforms they have
protected until now. Maebh is Clara's "gifted child",
scattering breadcrumbs as a gingerbread warning[21]

that Nature and future can treaty to deflect
the Nethersphere's ultimate
Designer.

---

[19] rebrand.ly/a0bvpx
[20] rebrand.ly/rmmcug
[21] rebrand.ly/bo3k97

Last Christmas

Once upon a dream – or on a rooftop –
there was Santa, or this saturated figure
posing as Santa, or Santa as a dream[22]

and his tangerines did not smell half
so sweet as Clara interrogating what
she thought must be reindeer CGI[23] props.

But then how do you tease fantasy apart
from reality when both are ridiculous?
Her dreams left voice for Danny, which

squared us in lies (Gallifrey's still out
there, tugging at time-warps for me
like the remixed words of a dead lover.)

Trust nothing.
Interrogate everything.

There are some things we should never
be OK about.

Those sleepers deep in your mind are
telepathic dream crabs[24] that can distract
you from nightmares with only an aftertaste

of ice-cream pain. *Just don't think
about them!* Pick out a manual number
at random to find out when you will

[22] rebrand.ly/ggccum
[23] rebrand.ly/uhftgw
[24] rebrand.ly/3uac9o

die in this dreamscape of avatars
as you cuddle the dream within
the dream that is Danny Pink

alive. Yes, it's complicated. Each of us
downloads our life into a memory bank
treating each deposit as our last

as we cling to Santa's sleigh above
our flickering notations of grey hair
and 62 years of LED regrets.

Trust nothing.
Interrogate everything.

There are some things we should never
proxy to our dreams.

Photo: unaffiliatedcritic.com

Series 9

Minerva: to Earthlings

You depict me as woman in the Capitoline[25]
but I am neither – and more powerful:
a deity of voice, freed by an intelligence
beyond decay, embedded in the nano
vacuum that siphons the breath of Jupiter.

Now, as I wait for the countdown,
I am your hope. I dare to gaze down
through the question marks that mist
a trio of booster rockets that will launch
me to the nearest exoplanet and its wobbling

star. My mission will over-dub the marble
of pantheon,[26] the atmosphere of speculation
that nudges brown dwarfs out of orbit.
This is no simulation: I am to dock
with the molten rains of Bellerophon[27]

on its dark side, of course – I'm a goddess,
not a martyr for hot Jupiters, and not about
to be tidally locked at 20000 C for scientists
long since dead to argue their theories.
Water and ozone are the atoms of poetry.

---

[25] rebrand.ly/qdxrmd
[26] rebrand.ly/b1jien
[27] rebrand.ly/7z5iyg

The Magician's Apprentice

Never mind those sucking Handmines:
if your chance to avoid their sinkholes[28]
is One in a Thousand, stack your chips

on the One, and I will save you
because that's what doctors do
even when I suspect you're just

Davros[29] in a boyish disguise.
Welcome to Class 'C' time where
Future second-guesses Past and no one

remembers which war we've landed in
amidst which planes and snipers can be
suspended in space by Time Lady

Missy who's very much "Not
Dead, Back, Big surprise", eager
to tease you with the Doctor's

Confession Dial,[30] to be decrypted
only after we're destroyed for all
time. 'Look for tiny anachronisms,'

she says of the Shadow Proclamation
as I soar my acidrockmetal guitar farewell
to the Dudes atop a medieval tank.

---

[28] rebrand.ly/l82k49
[29] rebrand.ly/nlfode
[30] rebrand.ly/ynuoqq

But Snakeface knows…remembers,
so we have to teleport to Planet Skaro
where Davros prattles via teleprompter

and I have to empathise to un-exterminate you.
But you and Missy have already shimmied
on solid space: the apprentice has learned

from an unexpected Master.

The Witch's Familiar

Clara seems so much taller
dangled by her ankles,
which is much more in your face

than being presumed dead by
Missy's gossip. While I, surrounded,
outnumbered, but then freed

from Snakeman's teleport thingy[31]
to outwit a mere babel of Android
assassins sans my sonic 'stick',

as Missy declaims it. I didn't think
I'd need it just to watch Davros die,
no tentacles prolonging his swansong.

His raspy words *almost* convinced me
this time he'd surrender his breath.
"Do me the courtesy," he says poshly,

"of actually *killing* me this time!" Is this
a bluff, or a counterbluff? I wonder.
Then "Why did you come?" he croaks.

"You're sick, and you asked," I reply.
He seemed so disarmed that instant
despite the debt of each and every

---

[31] rebrand.ly/df379y

Dalek to his life-force bubbling up
from the slime of their graveyard sewer[32]
to smear the survivors of their heart-

beats. "Tell me," he persists, "am I
a *good* man?" A curious chess move
from someone half Dalek, half Time Lord

tickling at my pity until Clara,
ensnared by Dalek-Speak,[33] begs for mercy.
Which I decrypt, thanks to my sporty sonic

glasses, and think maybe Davros
is right after all about unchained
love being a design flaw.

----

[32] rebrand.ly/qgsuro
[33] rebrand.ly/gtbcyt

Under the Lake

Ghosts? Never met one I couldn't tame,
until now. Just say boo from behind
your <u>sonic sunglasses</u>[34] and they

dissolve – or do they? But no, these
cosmic sailors hover, persistent,
curious, even. Who's in charge?

(I need to know which one I can ignore)
Meanwhile, everyone's abandoning
ship, or falling softly into death.

They can pass through walls, locked
doors, even <u>Clara's holographic double,</u>[35]
whispering the dark, the sound, the

forsaken temple, rewinding past, through
dark space from Orion's Nebula. I need maps,
precise coordinates to frame their positions,

a suspended animation chamber to see
how the slain relearn to hum, transmit
via some <u>Puppeteer's impossible magnet.</u>[36]

But then the flood, and Clara has to
trust me to teleport without the Tardis
and come back, ghost-free, to her

somehow.

———————

34 <u>rebrand.ly/343jlj</u>
35 <u>rebrand.ly/gn5svv</u>
36 <u>rebrand.ly/gyi7dn</u>

Heaven Sent

Where did all your floating skulls[37]
go wrong? You should know better
than to second-guess my worst dreams.

I have this thing about shovels. Especially
gardening. No one can sandcastle the second
of their birth or death. It's all about

diving, and holding your tainted breath
until the bubble-clues surface into answers.
Since the countdown never expires

I keep digging under the cracks in your
smile until I notice a second shadow
scanning my flashback of breadcrumbs.[38]

Suddenly the stars are out of kilter
And the planets are spinning in all
the wrong places. How many false starts

does it take to break through a wall harder
than diamonds[39] to Gallifrey – as the Veil's
bony fingers gasp me again and again?

At last the identity of the Hybrid is betrayed:
It's me: half Time Lord, half mortal, and I'm
determined not to regenerate an instant early.

Tell them I'm back –
And I'm coming!

[37] rebrand.ly/cq5ybc
[38] rebrand.ly/47s52a
[39] rebrand.ly/wou40o

The Husbands of River Song

Love may be even more circular than time
when it comes to husbands, which is why
the first in may also be the most lasting,

if not the best. My antlers are holographic[40]
in this silly season of detached regal heads
and my wish is for a bigger flowchart

of exoplanets saved and companions
jettisoned for their sake. King Hydroflax[41]
was River Song's third chapter, but he had this

fixation about head and diamond separation
that made romance a famine by jump cuts.
So my "Hello, Sweetie" was a kindly ace

though I never loved her back, even at Darillium's
Singing Towers, where her fictions of us
dissolved. At best it was a sunset of crystal

air where happy endings[42] are merely the lies
we tell ourselves in the dark hugs between
portals. Our slomo date of 24 years will just

have to divert.
Or do.

---

[40] rebrand.ly/75mf8a

[41] rebrand.ly/l04gsl

[42] rebrand.ly/k0rvnj

Photo: scifi.com

Series 10

Minerva: Wormholes

95

There's this part in *metastasis*[1]
when you throw a grenade in
and the wormhole turns orange

but then retreats back to green –
so what do you do?

Throw in two grenades
that'll destroy it…

Sorry, I was distracted
by chatter about some trailer
I've never played.

I really want to tell you about
black holes as time lords[2]
and the ultimate gasp

of holding on for dear death.
Here, or wherever we are when
there is here, space acts like a

fabric, watch it twist until
it can be measured, warping
space, until it loops into the past

entangling photons[3] into a future
surging faster than the speed of light.
Blue-sky thinking is the best when

we're far apart – or docking in a
fresh parallel. After all, what
we know about past and future

---

[1] rebrand.ly/k8usoo
[2] rebrand.ly/c9esv0
[3] rebrand.ly/v7522b

Photo: bbcamerica.com

The Pilot

How can you doubt that poetry and physics[4]
are the same? They almost rhyme except
when they don't but even then their tune

begs to be discovered. Most people
frown when they don't understand,
but you, dear Bill, smile so of course

I'm happy to be your personal tutor[5]
about time and life – its tidepools
and cinema of memories invented

frame by frame in our specs
that can be past, present, future –
at once. You are right to puzzle

how a puddle can be right there
when it hasn't rained for weeks
and how it can reflect or even

embody the lizard you imagine
in your brain when you confront
the pilot your Heather has become.

Never mind: she only wants to kill us!
Hardly anything or one is purely evil, just
hungry, dripping with that surplus of tears[6]

and we're at the wrong end of
her cutlery portal until you release her
from her sacred promise not to go.

---

[4] rebrand.ly/dpy873
[5] rebrand.ly/ws3lve
[6] rebrand.ly/2h0vdc

Thin Ice

History's mortgaged by the skaters,
those who elude the monster jaws
[sluicing the Thames](rebrand.ly/f4zms7)[7] with seductive

green searchlights and who live to tell
the collateral death of those who stood
inert at the weakest link and got dragged

under for a Master menu – nothing personal,
just random. Their gurgles will fall on deaf
ears because injustice can only appeal

when reason runs off to fight another
day. Have you heard of the 'stuff' that burns
underwater hotter then coal? There's hope

for ingenuity yet, but never underestimate
that collective human ability to [harness
the inexplicable](rebrand.ly/0a6psd).[8] Which is why I'm still

here, waiting for the snap thaw of
outrage, and the refrain of interstellar
space, which is why [I never steer](rebrand.ly/x09vxm)[9]

the Tardis, only roll with the angles
until my next episode (crisis)
blooms.

---

7 rebrand.ly/f4zms7
8 rebrand.ly/0a6psd
9 rebrand.ly/x09vxm

The Pyramid at the End of the World

Every trap

you walk into is
a chance to learn
where the laser points[10]

Power needs consent

so fake love is slavery[11]
hacking into sex

Watch the Doomsday Clock

tick away the pyramid
that undermines our fear

Being smart

is not
surrendering your planet[12]
for unconditional sight

---

[10] rebrand.ly/hl8ybc
[11] rebrand.ly/gfwpf6
[12] rebrand.ly/8mj94c

The Eaters of Light

They will keep chewing[13]
until no planets are left
or stars to navigate by

unless we can cave
the beast into a portal
for lost Romans[14] of the Light.

Damp crows at the gateway
to sunrise as my patience
shatters; the trouble with hope[15]

is resisting its music.

Photo: framerated.co.uk

---

[13] rebrand.ly/iobg1c
[14] rebrand.ly/xg3hk6
[15] rebrand.ly/tdzg8k

Twice Upon A Time

I have the game plan
to die again as a Doctor must
though something has grown

very wrong with the space
as I approach the chamber
of depleted Daleks[16]

We're no more than our
mistakes – ladies of glass,[17]
sons who mock their

fathers but a reconnected
life never hurt anyone, and
love is all the more networked

for memory on the long path
around. As my restless shadow
welcomes with feminine breath.[18]

[16] rebrand.ly/817b3
[17] rebrand.ly/f7su4o
[18] rebrand.ly/v9z357

Photo: bbc.co.uk

Series 11

Minerva: Second Genesis

We are ready to explore, decode
solar systems from <u>negative dust</u>[19]
deploy our spider-bots and drones

in our divining for maverick water,
carbon, understudy molecules.
As we <u>biomimic</u>[20] the voice between

silences, not distracted by ice-
whispers from <u>Comet 67P,</u>[21]
Rosetta arranges my samples

into sentient channels that zigzag
around black vacuums that
threaten with reckless energy.

It all boils down to puddles,
waveforms of future portals
shapeshifting before our eyes.

---

[19] rebrand.ly/2uievu
[20] rebrand.ly/oq2lfc
[21] rebrand.ly/yi6zym

Photo: uk.movies.yahoo.com

The Woman Who Fell to Earth

Once you learn how to tumble
from a bike you never forget.
Bad timing: I was in mid-transform[22]

from my grey-haired Scottish
skin (bless his sexy drawl!)
bracing for my train roof grand

entry, no time to muck about
with who I am or was or should be
though I do have this niggling

yearn for a certain runaway police-
box especially as I confront the data
coil of this flying spaghetti monster.[23]

Have I ever tasted a Hershey's Kiss?
Does it really matter as carriages uncouple
and Tzim-Sha[24] can zap us at will?

I do prefer the height-thrill of cranes
to the afterburn of virtual chocolate
as I blowtorch a fresh sonic screwdriver

from random scraps of metal. Damn
those budget cuts! We can do so much
better than purloined teeth for trophies.

Yes, always be *kind*!

---

[22] rebrand.ly/0k0xeh
[23] rebrand.ly/lqbzgj
[24] rebrand.ly/2xy7y0

The Ghost Monument

How do we know when a planet
is in the wrong place? A triad of suns
is a dead giveaway that we still

scatter in pythagorean squares.[25]
And how do we take up sides
when 3D monuments morph

into 4D operas?[26] Forget
my slippery gender: I still have
those two hearts even if my Tardis

has gone walkabout. Holographs[27]
are easy to trick when you're dancing
for/in time, but I prefer a locked door

tempting us with a cover song of fresh
challenges. It all comes down
to familiar air and options.

Right.
Let's get our shift on.

---

[25] rebrand.ly/j8p9dr
[26] rebrand.ly/i3e2oj
[27] rebrand.ly/4rs6iz

The Tsuranga Conundrum

The problem with junk galaxies is
their planets all look the same when
you trip over a sonic mine and then

get teleported into a remote controlled
hospital future sans exits but vibrations
in excess! Something's penetrated

our shields: a <u>muncher of non-organics</u>,[28]
Pting is pint-sized, almost cuddly, until
it snatches, chews and spits out my sonic

like granola, leaving it limp and smoking
to my disbelief. The toxic nerve of it!
Chief Medical Officer, Astos, is a bit

of a dish, but he gets jettisoned before
my second heart can even skip a beat
while some bloke is going into labour

without a <u>birth-bud</u>[29] after just three weeks'
gestation (his luck for not taking precautions!)
which is enough to spark my sonic back to life

and me to reflect on the joys of anti-
matter and how to lure <u>Pting</u>[30] to a dessert
of antimony – the ultimate energy gulp!

It all comes down to candy floss, Lego,
problem to be solved but mostly hope
as we pivot on worlds of imagination

ducking through asteroid showers

---

28 <u>rebrand.ly/fpwopj</u>

29 <u>rebrand.ly/fh6w8t</u>

30 <u>rebrand.ly/9swmnx</u>

Kerblam!

My Turkish hat surprise –
is it still me? Or some
encrypted HELP ME sob

slipping through the trip
wires of a macro marketeer?[31]
Still can't get into the swing

behind going organic and
though some of my best
enemies are robots I'm tempted

to bedevil these conveyor belts.[32]
Who can chill out when those
Group Loop eyes monitor

our every move? Kerblam
is such a well-oiled op
with a tailored box to suit

any wish – but loving my hat!
like Charlie and Kira, his 9 to 5
crush, so innocent smelling so

perfect – until she gets
confused down in the Triple 9s
mistaking that respect must run

both ways. *HELP ME* yet again
as we poke sticks in a wasp's
hive of conspiracy,[33] detected

[31] rebrand.ly/kex1y5
[32] rebrand.ly/z5xiud
[33] rebrand.ly/qebjdf

by Dispatch as organic
contaminates and rogue lip
reading. But isn't Twirlie

so hot? With synapses too
crowded to detect liquified
bombs in the bubblewrap.

The System's on auto-pilot
for naughty parcels counting
down to the final KERBLAM!

Teach you to play
with a stranger's bubblewrap,
Charlie!

Photo: imbd.com

Battle of Ranskoor AV

Dis-integrator of us all: how's that
for a planet not to be missed?
Just when I thought we'd learned

how little we actually can know,
the Tardis logs in no less than nine,
yes, nine urgent texts, so naturally

we have to trace them to source
where the fuss is all about unfinished
business and a dazed commander

who made the mistake of venturing
outdoors without a neurobalancer[34]
to calm his mind – and trigger

finger. It's 3407 years since their
'Creator' arrived, and the Ux[35]
are quite disarmed by his armour

and the fake truths he bristles
to keep them and those capsuled nine
planets in limbo, but I can disrobe

a demigod when I scan him
and those last seven years must
have really been a drag for T'zim-

Sha, hobbled by a stasis
of his own sketching, deadly
tentacles with consequences

---

[34] rebrand.ly/cz12x9
[35] rebrand.ly/sun7bl

for a High Noon with Graham
intent on [revenging his Grace](#)[36]
once their telepathic circuits

collide. And so the Universe
has a surprise in store: a shot
in the foot the final insult

sealing him hermetically in his
pride. Which reminds me:
have I mentioned that I half-

invented the Wellington?

Photo: pajiba.com

---

[36] [rebrand.ly/k25j07](#)

Series 12 (a taster)

Minerva: Pyrocene

My sensors have picked up surface flares
from the crust of a promising exoplanet
a mere 18796 light years away from our probe.

We have discounted the instigation of meteor
strikes but cannot rule out dry gasp thunder or
premeditation[37] by connatural or alien species.

If life resists there beyond the conflagration,
I trust that it will learn from the delicate
regeneration that Nature insists upon beyond

the eonic arrogance
of "intelligent"
beings.

---

[37] rebrand.ly/mijalb

Nikola Tesla's Night of Terror

No, this is not a tale of autonomous cars, but scorpion
invaders from Mars. I suppose Nikola had it coming
pinning his ear to the night waves. Then when he heard

a chatter of sorts, he had the brash to prattle back. He
should have known something was up from that pesky
Thassa Orb[1] spying on him mid-air with a greenish AC

but he was too busy inventing the 20th century
before that pretender Edison could cash in on his DC.
It wasn't just that Nikola reminded me of David Bowie

in that gilded New York City[2]: he also created alone,
in parentheses to the money-grabbers, too impatient
to let the world inch at a tortoise pace. But I digress:

The Queen of the Skithra wants to nab him before
he's recognised for being good at the impossible
(like me again!) Either he agrees to engineer her ship

or she'll Galli-fry Earth – a time-sensitive offer. He's
tempted. At least she's acknowledged his brilliance
and his sacrifice could be a legacy. Not on my watch!

Issuing Queenie with an airspace eviction notice
I give her one last chance to evolve. She refuses.
What else can you expect from a parasite with a kink

---

[1] rebrand.ly/bopvpg8
[2] rebrand.ly/lazqlsp

in her neck? Bring it on! While Yasmin decoys her Skithra hordes through the back alleys, we charge Nikola's Wardenclyffe Tower[3] with a bolt that zaps

the mother ship quicker than 5G – all in a day's doctoring! Poor Nikola dies penniless, but like I say you have to save Earth before you can change it.

Photo: denofgeek.com

---

[3] rebrand.ly/11v2r6g

Get the originals!

Paperback: bit.ly/3pZgR9r
eBook: bit.ly/338Ycij
Interactive Website: ipoz.biz/myplanets

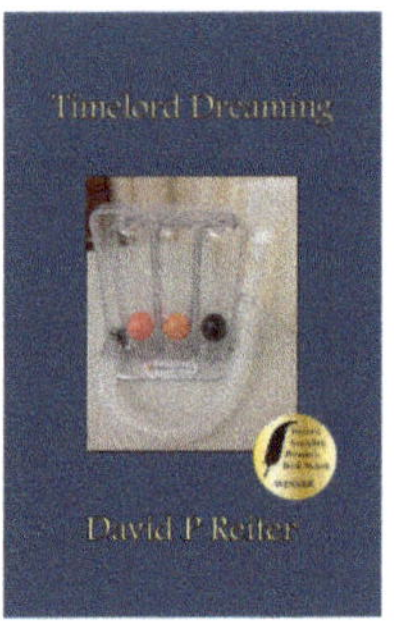

Paperback: bit.ly/3D8AbVm
eBook: bit.ly/3qUr2v3

Paperback: bit.ly/2u35ym2
eBook: bit.ly/2U34For
Audiobook: bit.ly/3hEXag9: